W9-CNA-833

Environment

in Focus

Waste Management

Cheryl Jakab

Marshall Cavendish
Benchmark
New York

This edition first published in 2011 in the United States of America by
Marshall Cavendish Benchmark
An imprint of Marshall Cavendish Corporation

Website: www.marshallcavendish.us

This publication represents the opinions and views of the author based on Cheryl Jakab's personal experience, knowledge, and research. The information in this book serves as a general guide only. The author and publisher have used their best efforts in preparing this book and disclaim liability rising directly and indirectly from the use and application of this book.

Other Marshall Cavendish Offices:
Marshall Cavendish International (Asia) Private Limited, 1 New Industrial Road, Singapore 536196 • Marshall Cavendish International (Thailand) Co Ltd. 253 Asoke, 12th Flr, Sukhumvit 21 Road, Klongtoey Nua, Wattana, Bangkok 10110, Thailand • Marshall Cavendish (Malaysia) Sdn Bhd, Times Subang, Lot 46, Subang Hi-Tech Industrial Park, Batu Tiga, 40000 Shah Alam, Selangor Darul Ehsan, Malaysia

Marshall Cavendish is a trademark of Times Publishing Limited

All websites were available and accurate when this book was sent to press.

Library of Congress Cataloging-in-Publication Data

Jakab, Cheryl.
  Waste management / Cheryl Jakab.
    p. cm. — (Environment in focus)
  Summary: "Discusses the environmental issue of waste management and how to
  create a sustainable way of living"—Provided by publisher.
  Includes bibliographical references and index.
  ISBN 978-1-60870-093-6
  1. Refuse and refuse disposal—Juvenile literature. I. Title.
  TD792.J345 2011
  363.72'8—dc22
                          2009042320

First published in 2010 by
MACMILLAN EDUCATION AUSTRALIA PTY LTD
15–19 Claremont Street, South Yarra 3141

Visit our website at www.macmillan.com.au or go directly to www.macmillanlibrary.com.au

Associated companies and representatives throughout the world.

Copyright © Cheryl Jakab 2010

Edited by Margaret Maher
Text and cover design by Cristina Neri, Canary Graphic Design
Page layout by Domenic Lauricella
Photo research by Sarah Johnson
Maps courtesy of Geo Atlas

Printed in the United States

Acknowledgments
The author and the publisher are grateful to the following for permission to reproduce copyright material:

Front cover photograph: Landfill, © Ralph125/iStockphoto

AAP Image/AFP, 26; © Momatiuk - Eastcott/CORBIS, 10; © Mark E. Gibson/CORBIS, 12;
© Martin Ruetschi/Keystone/CORBIS, 27; © Rick Maiman/Sygma/CORBIS, 6 (top), 9; © Paul Thompson/CORBIS, 16; Getty Images, 22; AFP/ Getty Images, 11; Tim Laman/Getty Images, 6 (bottom), 13; © Brasil2/iStockphoto, 5; © Lya Cattel/iStockphoto, 20, 24; © Chris Price/iStockphoto, 19; © Steve Cohen /Jupiter Images, 28 (left); © Image Source Black/Jupiter Images, 7 (bottom), 17; © Newspix / News Ltd / 3rd Party Managed Reproduction & Supply Rights, 29; Paul Rapson/SPL/Photolibrary, 14; REUTERS/Alexandra Beier, 15; REUTERS/John Javellana, 21; REUTERS/ Robin van Lonkhuijsen, 7, (top left), 23; REUTERS/Yuriko Nakao, 7 (top right), 25; © LianeM/Shutterstock, 18; © Monkey Business Images/ Shutterstock, 28 (right); © SergioZ/Shutterstock, 8.

While every care has been taken to trace and acknowledge copyright, the publisher tenders their apologies for any accidental infringement where copyright has proved untraceable. Where the attempt has been unsuccessful, the publisher welcomes information that would redress the situation.

Please note
At the time of printing, the Internet addresses appearing in this book were correct. Owing to the dynamic nature of the Internet, however, we cannot guarantee that all these addresses will remain correct.

135642

Contents

Glossary Words
When a word is printed in **bold**, you can look up its meaning in the Glossary on page 31.

Environment in Focus

Hi there! This is Earth speaking. Will you spare a moment to listen to me? I have some very important things to discuss.

We must focus on some urgent environmental problems! All living things depend on my environment, but the way you humans are living at the moment, I will not be able to keep looking after you.

The issues I am worried about are:
- large ecological footprints
- damage to natural wonders
- widespread pollution in the environment
- the release of **greenhouse gases** into the **atmosphere**
- poor management of waste
- environmental damage caused by food production

My challenge to you is to find a **sustainable** way of living. Read on to find out what people around the world are doing to try to help.

Fast Fact
Concerned people in local, national, and international groups are trying to understand how our way of life causes environmental problems. This important work helps us to learn how to live more sustainably now and in the future.

What's the Issue?
Waste Management

Waste is all the unwanted materials and substances that are left over from people's activities. It is often seen as a problem, something we have to get rid of. Today we need to understand that waste can be managed as a resource.

Waste as a Problem

Every year huge amounts of metal, glass, plastic, and **organic matter** are discarded as waste. Each of type of waste creates different problems. Many plastics do not break down easily or at all. **Biological waste** can cause disease or release harmful gases. Other waste, such as **electronic waste**, can release **pollutants**. Space for **landfill sites** or waste dumps has become extremely scarce.

Waste as a Resource

Managing waste as a resource means reusing or **recycling** all waste. The motto of waste management has long been "reduce, reuse, recycle." We can follow this motto to create zero waste.

Fast Fact
"Rethink" is sometimes added to the "reduce, reuse, recycle" motto for waste management. Today "resource" is also added, leading to the zero-waste motto: "Reduce, reuse, recycle, rethink, resource."

Many types of waste, such as cans, can be recycled and used as a resource.

Waste Management Issues

The most urgent waste management issues around the globe include:

- pollution from landfill sites
- increasing amounts of packaging
- lack of recycling of biological waste
- increased electronic waste
- the use of **incineration** to destroy waste

ARCTIC OCEAN

Arctic Circle

NORTH AMERICA

New York

NORTH ATLANTIC OCEAN

ISSUE 1

New York City
A landfill crisis highlights the need for better waste management. See pages 8–11.

Fast Fact
Some plastic materials disposed of as garbage do not break down for a very long time. They can last in the ground for thousands of years.

ISSUE 2

Bali
Litter from Bali's landfill is polluting the environment. See pages 12–15.

Around the Globe

ISSUE 5

Japan
Toxic fumes from incinerators are endangering people's health. See pages 24–27.

ISSUE 4

China
Incorrect disposal of dangerous electronic waste is damaging the environment and people's health. See pages 20–23.

A S I A

China

Japan

N O R T H

P A C I F I C

Tropic of Cancer

O C E A N

Equator

Bali

I N D I A N

O C E A N

AUSTRALIA

ISSUE 3

Australia
Human waste is being flushed down the toilet instead of being recycled. See pages 16–19.

Landfill Problems

The most common way of disposing of collected waste is dumping it into landfills. However, landfill areas create problems of odor, pollution, and pests. Rotting biological waste gives off greenhouse gases, such as **methane**, and can release polluting liquids into rivers and **groundwater**.

Space Problems

Available space for landfills is decreasing in many densely populated areas. Due to the lack of space in many cities, people often build housing on landfill sites after they have been filled. However, these areas have sometimes been heavily polluted by the waste dumped there. This pollution can cause health problems for people living on former landfill sites.

Fast Fact

In 2008, the city of Naples in southern Italy ran out of space in its landfills. All the city's garbage was taken on a 44-hour train trip to Hamburg, Germany. The waste was treated in Hamburg until new landfill sites and an incinerator were built in Naples.

Dumping waste into landfill sites creates huge piles of garbage.

The barge from Long Island sailed for five months trying to find a place to dump the garbage.

CASE STUDY

Long Island, New York

Long Island is an island located east of New York City. In 1987 a barge carrying garbage from Long Island traveled about 6,210 miles (10,000 kilometers) searching for a dump site. This crisis highlighted the problem of landfill and waste management in the area.

Long Island's Landfills

In the early 1980s, Long Island's landfills were a major source of groundwater pollution. A law was passed to stop all landfill by 1990. However, in 1987, about 80 percent of Long Island's garbage was still being dumped in landfills.

Sending Garbage Away

In 1987, Long Island's garbage was sent by barge to a dump in North Carolina. However, when the barge arrived, the community prevented the waste from being unloaded. The barge sailed to other ports, but no one would accept the waste. Finally, the garbage was returned to New York and incinerated.

Fast Fact
In 1905, three-quarters of the waste collected in New York City was coal ashes from fireplaces. Today the waste contains plastics, almost no ash, and much more paper.

Toward a Sustainable Future: Reducing Waste in Landfills

The amount of waste put into landfills can be greatly decreased. **Consumers** can reduce the amount of waste materials they discard and recycle waste wherever possible.

Reducing Materials

Consumers can reduce the amount of waste they produce by being careful shoppers. This means only buying what is really needed and replacing **long-life goods** less often. These simple actions reduce waste because fewer items end up being thrown away.

Manufacturers can also help by designing products to last longer. This reduces the number of long-life goods going to waste.

Recycling

Recycling reduces the amount of waste going to landfills. Using materials from recycled goods also reduces the need for new raw materials to be used in manufacturing. Waste-recycling services are now available in many regions. Most services require people to sort garbage into separate bins before collection.

Recycling centers now take many different materials which would have gone to landfills in the past.

Fast Fact
The organization Friends of the Earth states that at least 80 percent of our waste could be recycled.

waste*net* southland

RECYCLING CENTER

All Glass — Bottles / Jars
Paper — Newsprint
Cardboard — Flattened
Cans — Tin / Steel
Cans — Aluminium
Plastic Containers
Plastic Containers
Plastic — Milk Bottles
Plastic Containers

PLEASE WASH   PLEASE REMOVE LIDS   PLEASE REMOVE LIDS

For more information
Contact
Southland District Council
Phone (03) 218-7259
www.southlanddcwaste.govt.nz

Singapore's island of ash is now rich in biodiversity.

CASE STUDY
Landfill in Singapore

Since 1999 Singapore's only landfill has been an island made of ash.

Pulau Semakau Island

In 1998 Singapore's government built a 4-mile (7-km) long rock wall connecting two islands, Pulau Semakau and Pulau Sakeng. They began dumping ash from incinerated waste at the site. Over time, this has created a new island, also called Pulau Semakau.

Pulau Semakau now has coconut trees, banyan bushes, and grasses. The island also attracts rare species of animals. Visitors take guided tours to see the wildlife there.

Waste Disposal in Singapore

Since 1999, waste disposal companies in Singapore have been recycling glass, plastic, electronic waste, and even concrete. They incinerate what is left into ash. All of the incinerated waste from Singapore's 4.4 million residents is now dumped on Pulau Semakau.

Fast Fact
The Maldives began dumping its garbage directly into a lagoon on one of its small islands in 1992. This created the first-ever island made of waste.

11

The Increase in Packaging

Over the past hundred years packaging on goods has increased. Packaging is now the largest part of our waste. This is because packaging is usually designed to be thrown away once the contents are removed.

Why Have Packaging?

The main function of packaging is to protect the contents of the package from damage. Some packaging makes handling and transportation easier. It can also help prevent theft and make products look more attractive.

Packaging as Waste

Today, up to three-quarters of our waste is packaging. Most of this is put in landfills or burned. Despite public interest in recycling, at least a quarter of landfill space is taken up by glass, plastic, and cardboard packaging. These materials could be recycled. Many plastics are a long-term problem because they do not break down easily in landfills.

Fast Fact
In Britain, about 1.5 billion trash cans full of packaging go to landfills each year.

Packaging is necessary for some products, such as milk, but could be reduced on many others.

Litter from the TPA Suwung landfill near Denpasar, Bali, often ends up in nearby mangroves.

CASE STUDY
Litter in Bali

Bali is a popular Indonesian tourist destination. However, it is being littered with plastic bottles, bags, and other packaging as tourists discard their waste.

Garbage Collection

Any garbage that is collected on the island is taken to a landfill site outside Denpasar, Bali's capital. Trucks dump about 787 tons (800 tonnes) of food, plastic bags, and water bottles every day. Gases and leaks from the poorly managed landfill pollute the air and nearby mangroves.

Waste in Developing Countries

The poor waste management seen in Bali is common in **developing countries**. However, this is not simply lack of care. Garbage pickup and disposal can be too expensive for poorer governments. Tourist industries do not always take responsibility for visitors' garbage.

Fast Fact
In 2008, Italians were the world's biggest consumers of bottled water, drinking an average of 458 pints (260 liters) per person. This meant they also disposed of huge numbers of bottles, adding to waste problems.

13

Toward a Sustainable Future: Careful Packaging

It is impossible to get rid of packaging altogether. However, it can be greatly reduced on many products. It can also be made from sustainable materials.

Reducing Packaging

Many people around the world are encouraging manufacturers to reduce packaging on products. Manufacturers can also save money by reducing packaging. Sometimes there are good reasons for using packaging, such as health and safe handling. However, manufacturers need to avoid using packaging that is environmentally damaging or excessive.

Sustainable Packaging

Today, packaging can often be made from materials that are **biodegradable** or that can be recycled. For example, some plastics can now be broken down by bacteria or sunlight.

Fast Fact

In 2008, authorities in Venice, Italy, began giving visitors an empty drink bottle and a map showing the city's drinking fountains. They hope to stop people from buying bottled water, and to reduce the number of bottles discarded as waste.

Some plastics used in packaging are now biodegradable, such as this plastic that breaks down in compost.

The Green Dot, called der Grüne Punkt in German, is made up of black and green arrows inside a circle.

CASE STUDY
Green Dot Program

The Green Dot program was launched in Germany in 1991 to increase recycling. This system has reduced the amount of packaging manufacturers use and expanded the recycling industry.

How It Works

Companies pay to put the Green Dot logo on their packaging. The fee depends on the cost of recycling the materials in the packaging. The Green Dot fees pay for the collection and recycling of the packaging after it has been discarded.

Expanding the Program

Some ideas from Germany's program are now being adopted across the world. In European countries a law has been passed to increase recycling. The United Kingdom aims to have 92 percent of packaging recycled by 2010. Some manufacturing groups also support the idea of recycling schemes funded by manufacturers.

Fast Fact
In the United Kingdom, about 25 percent of household waste is recycled. In Switzerland, the Netherlands, and Germany about 60 percent is recycled, and in Flanders, Belgium, more than 70 percent.

Biological Waste

Almost all biological waste can be reused or recycled. However, most is discarded as unwanted or unsafe. This is a poor use of resources and adds to waste disposal problems.

What Is Biological Waste?

Biological waste is unwanted organic matter. For example, paper is a biological waste because it is made from wood. Biological waste includes human waste, or **excrement**, plant materials from home gardens or crops, and animal remains such as meat and bones. All biological waste is biodegradable.

What Happens to Biological Waste?

Biological waste that is collected as garbage is usually disposed of in landfills. Some people use **composting** to recycle some of the biological waste from their kitchen. Plant material, such as leaf litter and tree branches, can also be used as **mulch** on gardens. Human excrement is usually buried or discarded through **sewer systems.**

Most biological waste, including plant cuttings, can be recycled by composting.

Fast Fact

Organic matter is broken down by micro-organisms, such as fungi, molds, and bacteria.

Sewer treatment plants are used to treat human waste in most developed countries.

CASE STUDY
Flushing Human Waste Down the Toilet

ISSUE 3

In many **developed countries**, such as the United States, the toilet is the main way of removing human waste from buildings. In U.S. cities toilets are flushed with drinking-quality water.

Fast Fact
In 2005, the United Nations estimated that 4,000 children were dying each day from diseases carried in water.

Sewer Systems

Toilet contents are usually flushed into sewer systems, which take the excrement to **sewer treatment plants**. Removing excrement safely is important for human health, and the toilet is very effective at doing this. However, sewer systems use a great deal of water and do not create any usable products. The treated waste could be used as fertilizer. The water used could also be treated so it could be used again for drinking. However, in the United States and many other places these resources are not reused.

Toward a Sustainable Future: Recycling Biological Waste

Biological waste is now being collected and recycled as a resource in many communities around the world.

Treating and Recycling Human Waste

Huge volumes of human waste are created and must be treated every day. The treatment processes vary depending on the location. Recycling systems include composting toilets, toilets that do not use water, and waste-treatment plants that create usable water and fertilizer.

Energy from Biological Waste

As biological waste breaks down, it produces gases, such as methane. These gases can be used as a source of energy, called biogas. Biogas can be used as a fuel in electricity generators and boilers.

Fast Fact

In 2005, the city council of Toowoomba, Australia, proposed using treated sewer water for drinking. However, the plan was stopped. Even though treated water is pure, people believed it would be undesirable or unsafe to drink. They voted against the proposal.

Biogas plants are used to collect the methane produced by biological waste as it breaks down.

Food scraps in Alameda County can now be composted instead of being sent to landfills.

CASE STUDY

Alameda County Food-Waste Recycling

Since 2005, many people in Alameda County, California, have been able to send their food waste away for recycling.

Food-Waste Collection

In Alameda County, food waste and food-soiled paper, such as pizza boxes, are collected to be composted. Residents are given information about food-waste recycling and shown what to collect. They are also given a bucket with a lid for their food scraps.

The food scraps are collected weekly with residents' green-waste bins. The waste is then composted and used to enrich soils in landscaping and farming.

Waste Reductions

Before the program began, food scraps and food-soiled paper made up about 38 percent of the Alameda County's household waste. The county's target was to reduce the amount of waste sent to the landfill by 75 percent by 2010.

Electronic Waste

Electronic waste is made up of discarded electronic goods. Recycling of electronic goods is lagging well behind the rate of production. Many electronic waste items are disposed of incorrectly.

Electronic Goods

Electronic goods are devices that run on electricity or have electronic parts, such as washing machines, televisions, and computers. Manufacturers are constantly updating these items, so electronic goods quickly become outdated. When this happens, the goods are often replaced, even if the older model is still working. This increases waste because working goods are thrown out.

Disposal of Electronic Waste

Electronic waste is often disposed of incorrectly, such as by incineration, which releases dangerous fumes. Some electronic waste ends up in landfills. This can pollute the soil with materials that are harmful to human health, including lead, cadmium, and chromium.

Electronic waste is becoming a larger part of our garbage each year.

Fast Fact

A television can contain as much as 7.7 pounds (3.5 kilograms) of lead, a toxic metal. If disposed of incorrectly, this lead can make its way into groundwater and eventually into the water people drink.

Some people in Guiyu, China, collect electronic waste to extract the valuable metals it contains.

CASE STUDY
Exporting Electronic Waste

Much of the electronic waste produced in developed countries is exported to developing countries for dumping, reuse, or recycling. Guiyu, China, is a dumping ground for electronic waste.

Electronic Waste in Guiyu

In Guiyu, many people are involved in taking apart electronic waste to recover materials for recycling. This can be dangerous, since the people come into contact with poisonous substances. For example, plastic-coated electrical wires are burned to recover the copper inside. Circuit boards are heated to recover lead and washed with acid to recover gold. These activities release chemicals that damage people's health and the environment.

Banning Imports of Electronic Waste

In 2004, the Chinese government banned electronic-waste imports. However, electronic waste is still being imported illegally.

Fast Fact

As electronic-waste imports are banned from some countries, they are being smuggled into others. This includes many developing countries in Asia and parts of Africa.

Toward a Sustainable Future: Recycling Electronic Waste

Electronic waste can be recycled to obtain valuable resources. This can be done using methods that are safe for people and the environment.

Resources from Recycling

Many materials in electronic goods can be recycled for use in other products. In an average television there is steel, aluminum, and copper that can be recycled again and again. Computers contain small amounts of gold and silver. These can be recycled at a lower cost than mining new metals. Even plastic can be recycled.

Safe Recycling

There are now businesses that recycle electronic goods safely. Rather than mining metals from the ground, the recycling companies "mine" the valuable parts from the devices. Safety equipment and safe work methods are used to protect workers from hazards.

Fast Fact
The U.S. Environmental Protection Agency estimates that 1.7 million tons (1.8 million t) of electronic waste goes into landfills in the United States each year.

Electronic waste can be recycled safely when the correct equipment and methods are used.

Greenpeace is urging the electronics company Philips to introduce voluntary take-back plans.

CASE STUDY

End-of-Life Take-Back Plans

Electronic waste can be recycled through end-of-life take-back plans. These plans encourage electronics companies to take back products at the end of their useful life. The companies make sure the parts are safely recycled.

Voluntary Take-Back Plans

Some electronics companies, such as Sony, Samsung, and Nokia, have voluntary take-back plans. They take back products even in countries where they are not required to do so by law.

Who Should Pay for Recycling?

Some electronics companies do not want to pay for the recycling of their products. They want consumers to pay a recycling fee instead. Greenpeace campaigners say end-of-life take-back plans are the only way to make sure electronic products are disposed of safely.

Fast Fact

In 2009, Greenpeace found that electronic waste was being sent from the United Kingdom to Nigeria. The waste had been intended for safe recycling, but instead was disguised as second-hand goods and exported illegally.

Incinerating Waste

Some waste cannot be recycled, so incinerators are used to transform it into energy. However, these incinerators can also cause problems.

Incinerator Problems

Incinerators that burn waste materials produce a great deal of heat. This can be captured as an energy source. However, dangerous gases, which may cause health problems, can be released from old or poorly designed incinerators.

Sorting Waste

One of the biggest problems with waste incinerators is poorly sorted waste. If waste is not properly sorted, recyclable materials are not removed before the waste is burned. Burning recyclable materials is a waste of valuable resources. Materials such as plastics can also create dangerous gases when incinerated in the wrong conditions.

Gases released from incinerators are not always monitored, and can contain harmful substances.

Fast Fact

Each year people produce at least 2.4 billion tons (2.5 billion t) of waste. This is more than all the grains grown worldwide.

Japanese workers check waste that is sent to incinerators to remove recyclable materials.

CASE STUDY
Waste Incinerators in Japan

Japan has more waste incinerators than any other country in the world. About three-quarters of all solid waste produced in Japan is burned.

Japan's Waste

On average, people in Japan each produce more than 2 pounds (1 kg) of waste per day. However, there is not much room for landfill sites in Japan. To dispose of waste, the Japanese began to use incinerators as their population grew.

Much of the waste is sorted before it is incinerated to remove recyclable materials, such as plastics. However, a great deal of valuable recyclable material is still incinerated.

Fast Fact
Japan has more than 1,800 incinerators burning 49 million tons (50 million t) of waste each year.

Pollution from Incinerators

Many of Japan's older and smaller incinerators are polluting the air with toxic chemicals. These include chemicals called dioxins. Dioxins have been linked with many health problems, including cancer, birth defects, and liver damage.

Toward a Sustainable Future: Waste Mining

For a sustainable future, waste can be "mined" for the resources it contains. Waste mining takes resources from waste to generate energy, provide fertilizer, or to be reused in new items. Ideally, all of the waste would be used, to leave us with zero waste.

Zero Waste

The environmental group Greenpeace is supporting zero waste as the target for a sustainable future. Currently, most waste is still disposed of in landfill or by incineration. To reach zero waste all waste would need to be reused or recycled.

Clean Development Mechanism

The United Nations Clean Development Mechanism helps developing countries to control all forms of pollution, including waste. It helps developing countries to get money to install equipment that collects energy from waste. For example, waste in landfills produces polluting gases. However, these gases can be captured. They can then be used to generate electricity.

This equipment in Norway uses methane collected from waste to produce electricity.

Fast Fact
Kamikatsu province in Japan is planning for zero waste by 2020.

Some mechanical biological treatment plants use water to help break down biological waste.

CASE STUDY

Mechanical Biological Treatment

Mechanical biological treatment (MBT) will soon be used to treat waste in Lancashire, in the United Kingdom. MBT "mines" the resources from waste using two steps, a mechanical step and a biological step.

Mechanical Step

The mechanical step removes solid wastes such as metal, plastic, and glass. Different mechanisms separate the different kinds of waste for recycling. For example, air jets blow different types of plastic into separate bins. The remaining waste is sorted by hand to remove any toxic materials.

Biological Step

During the biological step, the biological waste is washed and air is added. This removes any remaining pieces of metal, plastic, and glass. The sludge that is left is broken down by bacteria to produce methane. The methane is used as the energy source to run the recycling plant. The remaining organic matter is composted and used as fertilizer in tree plantations.

What Can You Do? Consume Less and Reduce Waste

Recycling changes waste into a resource. However, it is even better to consume less and create less waste in the first place. You could try some of the following ideas to reduce your consumption.

Keep an Activity Log

Keep a log of your activities for a day. Record where you could reduce consumption. Reducing your consumption mainly involves thinking about what you are doing as you do it.

Make No-Waste Lunches

Each day, school lunches produce garbage, but they do not have to. You can avoid using plastic and disposable packaging. After you have eaten, you can compost any leftover food scraps. You can even talk to your teacher about setting up a compost bin at school.

Fast Fact
A lunch that contains fresh fruit and vegetables rather than fruit juice packs and stewed fruit containers is healthier and reduces packaging.

School lunches can be packed without using plastic wrap to create a no-waste lunch.

You can take reusable shopping bags to the supermarket instead of using plastic bags.

Reduce Your Use of Plastic Bags

Plastic shopping bags have become common garbage items. You can try to reduce your use of these bags.

Keep a log of all the plastic bags your family uses in a week. Also list the times when they avoided using a plastic bag. After that week:

- List the ways you have reduced your family's use of plastic bags.
- List the ways your family members could further reduce their use of plastic bags.

Create a poster to show how the use of plastic bags can be reduced. Display your poster at home or at school.

One way to reduce your use of plastic bags is to take reusable bags when you shop. Think about ways to remind your family to use them. For example, you could design and make a reminder note to hang on your refrigerator.

Fast Fact
Recycling helps prevent global warming by reducing the amount of energy used to produce new materials.

Toward a Sustainable Future

Well, I hope you now see that if you take up my challenge your world will be a better place. There are many ways to work toward a sustainable future. Imagine a world with:

- a sustainable ecological footprint
- places of natural heritage protected for the future
- no more environmental pollution
- less greenhouse gas in the air, reducing global warming
- zero waste and efficient use of resources
- a secure food supply for all

This is what you can achieve if you work together with my natural systems.

We must work together to live sustainably. That will mean a better environment and a better life for all living things on Earth, now and in the future.

Websites

For further information on managing waste, visit the following websites.

- EPA Waste Management www.epa.gov/osw/
- Greenpeace www.greenpeace.org.uk/toxics/solutions
- Earth 911 http://earth911.com
- Emergo Europe Green Dot information www.greendotcompliance.eu/en/about-green-dot.php

atmosphere
The layers of gases surrounding Earth.

biodegradable
Able to be broken down by bacteria and other organisms.

biological waste
Unwanted organic matter, such as lawn clippings.

composting
Allowing organic matter to decompose, leaving a rich source of nutrients.

consumers
People who use or consume resources.

developed countries
Countries with industrial development, a strong economy, and a high standard of living.

developing countries
Countries with less developed industry, a poor economy, and a lower standard of living.

electronic waste
Waste from pieces of equipment that run by electricity.

excrement
Waste removed from the bodies of living things.

greenhouse gases
Gases that help trap heat in Earth's atmosphere.

groundwater
Water found below the surface of the land.

incineration
Burning at high temperatures.

landfill sites
Areas of land where waste is dumped.

long-life goods
Products such as computers that are kept for a number of years.

methane
A gas that is given off from burning fossil fuels and decomposing vegetation, including the digestion of plants by animals.

mulch
Organic material, such as straw, used to cover soils.

organic matter
Material from living things.

pollutants
Any unwanted substances in the environment.

recycling
Reprocessing a material so that it can be used again.

sewer systems
Systems that carry away and treat human waste.

sewer treatment plants
Areas where human waste is made safe by a range of chemical and biological processes.

sustainable
Does not use more resources than Earth can regenerate.

Index